NICKELODEON

The BACKYARDIGANS

Rain, Rain, Go Away

adapted by Catherine Lukas

based on the screenplay "Match on Mt. Olympus" written by Robert Scull

illustrated by Susan Hall

SIMON SPOTLIGHT/NICKELODEON
New York   London   Toronto   Sydney

Based on the TV series *Nick Jr. The Backyardigans*™ as seen on Nick Jr.®

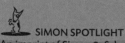
SIMON SPOTLIGHT
An imprint of Simon & Schuster Children's Publishing Division
1230 Avenue of the Americas, New York, New York 10020
© 2010 Viacom International Inc. All rights reserved. NICK JR.,
Nick Jr. The Backyardigans, and all related titles, logos, and characters
are trademarks of Viacom International Inc. NELVANA™ Nelvana Limited.
CORUS™ Corus Entertainment Inc. All rights reserved.
All rights reserved, including the right of reproduction in whole or in part in any form.
SIMON SPOTLIGHT and colophon are registered trademarks of Simon & Schuster, Inc.
For information about special discounts for bulk purchases, please contact
Simon & Schuster Sales at 1-866-506-1949 or business@simonandschuster.com.
Manufactured in the United States of America, 0110 LAK
First Edition 10 9 8 7 6 5 4 3 2 1
ISBN 978-1-4169-8509-9

"I'm Weatherman Tyrone," said Tyrone, "reporting on the weather for all of Ancient Greece. Today is going to be sunny and beautiful, without a cloud in the sky. Now, over to Pablo, who will bring us the news in sports!"

"Thanks, Tyrone. I'm Sportscaster Pablo," said Pablo. "Today is a great day to play basketball! So let's get outside and play. Well, that's all for now. Thanks for watching!"

Tyrone and Pablo headed outside to play some basketball.

"Great sports broadcast, Pablo," said Tyrone.

"Thanks," said Pablo. "You did a great job reporting the weather. Here, catch!" he added.

Tyrone caught the basketball and dribbled it.

Suddenly lightning flashed and thunder clapped. Rain poured down.

"Hey!" said Pablo. "I thought you said the weather was going to be sunny today!"

Tyrone shrugged. "I don't control the weather. I just report it. The goddess of weather controls the rain. She lives up there." He pointed toward Mt. Olympus in the distance.

"Well, let's just go up to Mt. Olympus and ask the goddess to make it stop!" said Pablo.

"We can't do that! We might make her angry!" said Tyrone.

"Aw, come on. It can't hurt to ask," said Pablo.

"We should at least bring an offering," said Tyrone. "Greek goddesses like presents."

"Good idea! We can teach her how to play basketball!" said Pablo.

"Yeah, let's go!" Tyrone said, and off they went to Mt. Olympus.

"Gee, it's sunny up here above the clouds!" said Pablo. "Let's find the goddess of weather so we can stop the rain on Earth and get back to our game," said Tyrone.

Pablo passed the ball to Tyrone, who began dribbling it. Suddenly they heard something in the distance.

"Ha! Ha! Ha! Ha!" came a booming voice.

"He doesn't look like the goddess of weather to me," whispered Tyrone. "Let's get out of here before he sees us."

"Halt!" said the voice. "I am Austin, the god of laughter! I command you to laugh!"

ZAP!

Suddenly Tyrone began laughing uncontrollably. "Ha! Ha! Ha! Run, Pablo! Ha! Ha!" said Tyrone.

"Now I will make *you* laugh until milk comes out of your nose!" shouted Austin, chasing after Pablo.

Pablo skidded to a stop and whirled around to face Austin. "Wait!" he shouted. "I bring you an offering!"

"What's that?" asked Austin, staring suspiciously at Pablo's basketball.

"It's a basketball. My friend and I can teach you how to play."

Austin snapped his fingers, and Tyrone stopped laughing. Then Tyrone and Pablo taught Austin how to play basketball.

"Wow!" said Austin, laughing as he dribbled the ball. "Basketball is my new favorite sport! Thanks for teaching me!"

"You're welcome," said Pablo. "Now we have to go find the goddess of weather and ask her to make it stop raining down on Earth."

Austin rolled his eyes. "Well, be careful. She's not very nice," he said.

They tiptoed past a sleeping goddess.
"Is *that* the goddess of weather?" whispered Tyrone.
Pablo shook his head. "I don't think so," he whispered back.

The goddess opened her eyes and sat up. "Who disturbs my nap? I am Uniqua, the goddess of naps!" She saw Tyrone, and before he could move—*ZAP!*—she sprinkled magic sleepy dust on him.

Tyrone fell into a deep sleep.

"And now I will make *you* snooze too!" Uniqua said to Pablo.
Pablo ducked out of the way just in time.
"Wait!" he shouted. "We brought you an offering!"
"Well, what is it?" asked Uniqua suspiciously.
"If you wake up my friend, we'll teach you to play a new game,"
he said.
"I like games!" she hollered. "Show me!"

Uniqua waved her hand and Tyrone woke up. Pablo and Tyrone showed her how to play basketball. Before long, she was dunking the ball and passing it to Tyrone.

"This is fun!" she said. "Thanks for teaching me how to play!"

"Can you tell us how to find the goddess of weather?" asked Pablo. "We need to ask her to make it stop raining down on Earth."

Uniqua frowned. "She's always busy, and she never takes a nap. Maybe that's why she's so cranky. If you really want to find her, go that way. But be careful."

Once they reached the gate to the goddess of weather's palace, they heard thunder, lightning, and lots of muttering.

"Whoa," said Pablo.
"Whoa is right," agreed Tyrone as they climbed the stairs.
At the top of the stairs, Tasha, the goddess of weather, was looking at a giant globe.

Pablo cleared his throat. "Um, excuse me, but we were hoping you could make it stop raining on Earth," he said.

The goddess of weather turned to see who was there. "I'll make it rain if I want to!" she said. "Now, go away! I'm busy. This is a serious job, controlling whether it will rain or shine."

"Could we, um, interest you in taking a little break? To play some basketball?" asked Pablo meekly.

"I said I'm busy. Didn't you hear me?" she grumbled. Then, a sly smile spread across the goddess of weather's face. "Basketball, huh?"
Tasha picked up her giant globe to use as a basketball. *CRASH! FLASH!* With a wave of her hand, she created a basketball court.

She dribbled the globe expertly around her legs, flipped it into the air, caught it, and took a jump shot. *SWISH!*

Pablo and Tyrone looked at each other. They both gulped.

"No one can beat *me* at basketball!" said Tasha.

"Oh, really?" said a voice. "You want to bet on that?"

Goddess Tasha stared. It was the goddess of naps and the god of laughter. "You know how to play basketball?" Tasha asked.

"Yeah. Pablo and Tyrone taught us!" said Austin. "So, let's play all of us against you."

"What should we bet?" asked Tasha.

Pablo spoke up. "If we win, you make it stop raining down on Earth!" he said.

"Hmm," said Tasha. "Okay, but if I win, I will make it rain . . . forever! The first team to score a basket wins!"

Pablo and Tyrone gulped again.

They played hard. Austin caught the ball.
"I'm open!" yelled Pablo.
"I'm open too!" said Tyrone.
Austin passed the ball. Pablo and Tyrone looked up.
The giant basketball was right overhead.
"Uh-oh!" they both said.
FWUMP!

The three gods stared at where Pablo and Tyrone had just disappeared beneath the ball.

Suddenly the ball quivered . . . flew high up into the air, and sailed directly toward the basketball hoop.

"Noooooo!" yelled Tasha as she lunged for the ball, but it was too late.

SWISH! It went into the basket! "We won! We won!" yelled Tyrone, Pablo, Uniqua, and Austin.

They all tumbled back down to Earth. Tasha kept her word and stopped the rain . . . just in time for the afternoon weather report.

"It's going to be a sunny afternoon," Weatherman Tyrone said, "thanks to Goddess Tasha."

"Sure is perfect weather for a basketball game," said Sportscaster Pablo, "Wait a second! Did I just hear thunder?"

"That wasn't thunder," said Tasha with a grin. "That was my stomach rumbling! I'm hungry for a snack!"

"Let's go to my house for some Greek pastries!" said Pablo.

"And some basketball!" said Tyrone. And they all headed to Pablo's house for a snack and a game.